# ISLAND OF LOST MASKS

# By Ryder Windham

Scholastic Inc.

LEGO, the LEGO logo, and BIONICLE are trademarks of the LEGO Group. © 2015 The LEGO Group. Produced by Scholastic Inc. under license from the LEGO Group.

ISBN 978-0-545-87325-3

10 9 8 7 6 5 4 3 2 1     15 16 17 18 19

Printed in the U.S.A.     40

First printing 2015

Book design by Erin McMahon

# CHAPTER 1

## THE HEROES ARRIVE

**When the young boy** saw the skull spiders skittering toward him, he screamed and accidentally dropped the long stick he'd been carrying as a weapon before he turned and started running for his life. The spiders' sharp-tipped legs stabbed into the ground, leaving trails of holes in the jungle mountain's foothills. The boy ran up a path along the edge of a cliff, heading for the woods. He was hoping he could make it to his hiding place when he saw more skull spiders ahead of him, blocking his way. He came to a quick stop.

Like all the people on the vast island of Okoto, the boy wore a sacred mask. Unable to move forward or back, he realized his only choice to escape the spiders was to jump off the cliff. As the spiders moved closer, he trembled and clutched the edges of his mask and cried, "Help!"

The boy jumped in surprise as a powerful blast of sand smashed into the spiders behind him. The blast knocked the spiders off the path and over the edge of the cliff, and they screeched as they fell. Wondering about the source of the blast, the boy turned quickly and saw an armored warrior running up the path from below.

The warrior wore a brown mask and held a staff-like weapon with two glowing ends, and

2

he shouted, "Duck!" The boy dropped to a crouch while the warrior, still running, fired again and again, volleying blasts of sand that sailed over the boy's body. The sand crashed against the spiders on the upper trail, and they screeched as they, too, went over the cliff's edge.

The warrior came to a stop beside the boy. "Are you all right?"

The boy gasped as he stood up. "Yes. Thank you!"

The warrior bowed his head slightly. The boy pointed to the warrior's weapon and said, "You . . . you are Nilkuu, the Protector of Stone! My father told me stories about you and your sandstone blaster. I am Bingzak."

Nilkuu looked around, scanning the area for any sign of danger. "Bingzak, why are you here, so far from the nearest village?"

"My village is gone, destroyed by the skull spiders! I alone escaped with my mask. I have been hiding in the jungle ever since."

Nilkuu shook his head sadly. "I am sorry, Bingzak. This is a dark time for our island. Many have lost their masks to the skull spiders and fallen under the control of the Lord of Skull Spiders."

"May I ask why you are not now in the Stone Region?"

"I have traveled to the Jungle Region for an important mission. I must get to the Temple of Time immediately."

"The Temple of Time?" Confused, Bingzak said, "But . . . if you wound up here, you must have taken a wrong turn on the mountain trail. Are you lost?"

Nilkuu snorted through his mask. "Of course not. Protectors never get lost."

"Never?"

"Well, almost never. It is not often that I leave the Region of Stone. Also, this jungle is so full of trees that look the same to me."

"I can guide you to the temple." Bingzak pointed to the woods. "I know a shortcut."

Nilkuu thought for a moment, then said, "It would be wrong of me to leave you here alone. It would be best if you accompanied me to the temple."

"Come on, it's this way." Bingzak started walking toward the woods. Nilkuu followed.

Darkness began to fall across the island, making distant stars and other planets visible in the sky. Nilkuu and Bingzak proceeded past towering trees, across a mountain stream, and up a steep slope until they arrived at a clearing. In the middle of the clearing, silhouetted against the sky, stood the Temple of Time. The temple resembled an enormous metronome, complete with a long pendulum that made a rhythmic ticking noise as it rocked back and forth from its pivot point at the base of the temple's foundation.

Five warriors stood outside the temple's entrance. They wore similar armor and masks, but each was distinguished by a different color and carried unique weapons. Bingzak immediately recognized the green-masked warrior as Vizuna, Protector of Jungle, and realized the other warriors were also Protectors. Izotor, Protector of Ice, wore a white mask and held an ice saw. Kivoda, Protector of Water, wore a blue mask, and had two water-propulsion turbines secured to his back. Korgot, Protector of Earth, wore a mask of dark purple and carried a large, star-shaped drill. And the red-masked warrior was Narmoto, Protector of Fire, who carried two flame swords.

An astonished Bingzak said, "All six Protectors of Okoto? Gathered together in one place?" Looking at Nilkuu, he added, "When you told me your mission was important, you weren't kidding!"

As Nilkuu and Bingzak approached the temple, the Protector of Ice said, "You're late, Nilkuu. Did you get lost?"

Before Nilkuu could reply, Bingzak said, "The Protector of Stone was not lost! He was delayed because he rescued me from skull spiders!"

"I know this boy," said Vizuna. "He is from a nearby village." Facing Bingzak, Vizuna added, "I am relieved to see you are okay."

Nilkuu gestured to Bingzak and said, "He was alone when I found him. I brought him here to keep him safe."

"No one on Okoto will be safe unless we fulfill our mission," said the Protector of Fire.

Nilkuu turned to Bingzak and said, "You must remain here. Wait for me."

Leaving Bingzak, Nilkuu followed the other Protectors into the Temple of Time. Once inside, the Protectors opened a vault to remove the Mask of Time and brought the mask to an open area that was exposed to the night sky. At the center of the area was a pool of mystical light. After they placed the mask in the pool, they gathered in a circle around it. The Protector of Water said, "Now we must recite the Prophecy of Heroes."

The Protectors spoke in unison:

*"When times are dark and all hope seems lost, the Protectors must unite. One from each tribe.*

*"Evoke the power of past and future and look to the skies for an answer.*

*"When the stars align, six comets will bring*

*timeless heroes to claim the Masks of Power and find the Mask Maker.*

*"United, the elements hold the power to defeat evil. United but not one."*

Within the pool that held the Mask of Time, the light swirled and became brighter, igniting a brilliant beam that projected up from the temple and into the sky. Several seconds later, the beam vanished, leaving the Protectors in darkness.

Blinking his eyes, Nilkuu said, "Did it work?"

"The Prophecy *must* work," said the Protector of Fire. "It is our only hope to defeat the evil forces that have risen from our island."

Nilkuu said, "What happens next?"

"We return to our regions," said the Protector of Earth, "and we do all that we can to defend our tribes as we wait for the stars to align. And for the well-being of all, let us hope the comets come sooner than later."

After placing the Mask of Time back in its vault, the six Protectors exited the temple. Outside, Nilkuu found Bingzak waiting and bent down beside him. Nilkuu whispered, "Thank you for not letting the others know that I may have gotten lost in the jungle."

"Well, you did save my life!" Nilkuu said.

Nilkuu gazed up at the stars overhead. "I must go back to the Region of Stone. I hope I won't take a wrong turn again."

Bingzak cleared his throat. "Protector of Stone, I have no reason to remain here. I would be honored if you allowed me to guide you . . . I mean, to *accompany* you to the Region of Stone."

Nilkuu rose to his feet. "That is very generous of you. I'll take you up on that offer."

"Great!" said Bingzak. "Come on! Let's get going!"

# ᴄᴇᴡᴀ

Days later, in a fortress village of the Stone Protector in the Region of Stone, Nilkuu and Bingzak were standing with members of the Stone tribe on the roof of the fortress. The roof was lined with a low, protective wall with battlements—openings that offered a wide view of the surrounding desert and also provided protective cover for the village's sentries. The sentries were armed with swords and long spears. Bingzak had been helping Nilkuu and the sentries watch out for skull spiders when he looked up at the night sky and said, "I didn't know you could see different stars from here."

"Different stars?" said Nilkuu. "What do you mean?"

"Back in the Jungle Region, I never saw that constellation." Bingzak pointed to a cluster of six bright points of light overhead. "That's strange. The constellation is . . . moving!"

Behind his mask, Nilkuu's eyes went wide. "That's no constellation." He turned to the sentries and said, "The comets have arrived. They're falling to Okoto!"

The villagers looked to the sky just as the comets appeared to break formation, moving away from one another so that each was falling toward a different area of the island. Nilkuu watched one comet grow brighter as it angled over the desert. The comet plummeted toward a rocky plateau to the east of the fortress and exploded in a bright flash, releasing a shock wave that lifted several sentries off their feet and across the open roof.

Nilkuu grabbed Bingzak and pulled him behind a protective wall until the shock wave passed. "Stay here with the sentries," Nilkuu said. Taking his sandstone blaster with him, Nilkuu leaped over the battlements and fell away from the fortress. Landing on the hard-packed sand, he sprinted for the plateau where the comet had come to rest.

White smoke was still billowing up from the comet's scorched rubble when Nilkuu arrived at the plateau. A tall, shadowy figure rose away from the debris, stepped forward, and emerged from the smoke. Nilkuu saw a brown mask, the same color as the mask worn by Nilkuu, covered the figure's face. The figure carried a long dagger and a pair of curved throwing weapons that Nilkuu recognized as legendary stormerangs, which could generate sandstorms along their path.

The figure rubbed the back of his head. Sounding slightly dazed, he said, "What happened? Where am I?"

Nilkuu bowed. "Welcome, Pohatu, Master of Stone, to the island of Okoto. I am Nilkuu, the Protector of Stone."

Pohatu stopped rubbing his head, looked down at Nilkuu, and then turned his head fast to look behind him. Returning his attention to Nilkuu, he said, "You're, *umm*... You're talking to me?"

"Yes, Pohatu."

*"Hmm."* Pohatu shook his head. "I never heard the name *Pohato* before. Never heard of this island, either. Actually, now that I think of it, I can't say I remember ... anything."

Confused, Nilkuu said, "Um, Poha*tu* ... You don't know about the Prophecy of Heroes? That you're one of six heroes, delivered here by comets? It is your destiny to defeat evil and save our island from—?"

A loud horn sounded over the desert, interrupting Nilkuu and prompting him to look back at the fortress. "That's the fortress alarm. Skull spiders are attacking the village!"

"Skull spiders?"

"No time to explain!" Nilkuu said as he started running back to the fortress. He'd covered only a small stretch of ground when he felt an incredible rush of wind from behind, and then something grabbed the armor at his back and lifted him high into the air. Craning his neck, he saw Pohatu had taken hold of him, and also saw a small tornado whipping around Pohatu's lower body.

"The legends are true!" Nilkuu said as they rose higher and moved fast toward the fortress. "You can fly!"

"Stop squirming," Pohatu said.

Nilkuu looked down and saw that they had already arrived over the fortress. Skull spiders were clambering up the fortress's outer walls, and the sentries were thrusting spears at the spiders, desperately trying to knock them down. One spider scurried past the sentries and snuck up behind Bingzak. Bingzak screamed as the spider pounced on him and clamped its body over the boy's head and mask.

Pohatu released Nilkuu, letting him fall so that he landed a short distance from Bingzak, just as the boy picked up a fallen spear and moved to attack the sentries. Nilkuu knew that Bingzak was not himself, that his mind and body had fallen completely under the control of the Lord of Skull Spiders. Nilkuu drew his sandstone blaster and fired at the spider that covered Bingzak's head. The spider screeched and then fell away from Bingzak, who collapsed against the roof. Using its remaining legs, the spider jumped through an opening in the battlements. Nilkuu ran to the opening and looked down. He saw dozens of spiders crawling up and across the outer wall of the fortress.

Still elevated above the fortress, Pohatu angled the swirling base of his tornado toward the spiders on one outer wall, and then he began to circle the structure. Unable to escape the power of the vortex, the spiders were torn from the wall and swept into the tornado, which then sent them soaring away from the fortress. One by one, the spiders fell with skeleton-shattering impact onto the rocky plateau. The sentries cheered.

Nilkuu knelt beside Bingzak and said, "Are you all right?"

Bingzak groaned as he rubbed his mask. "I think so. But ... I remember it was terrible! The Lord of Skull Spiders took over my mind!"

"Relax, boy," Nilkuu said. "You're safe now."

Pohatu guided his tornado into a steep descent and landed near Nilkuu. As Nilkuu rose away from Bingzak, Pohatu said, "Did I not defeat evil?"

"You're off to a good start," Nilkuu said, "but the Lord of Skull Spiders nearly took permanent possession of this boy." He gestured to Bingzak.

"Please explain."

"The Lord of Skull Spiders controls all skull spiders on the island. When he gains an islander's mask, he also gains control of that islander. Many islanders have been lost to us, and the evil is rising."

Pohatu said, "Are you certain I am here to defeat evil?"

Nilkuu nodded. "According to the Prophecy, six heroes, the Toa, will arrive on the island.

Each will go on a quest for Golden Masks to unlock their great powers. To find your mask, we must journey to the Shrine of the Mask of Stone."

Pohatu gazed out across the desert. "When do I begin this quest?"

"Right now."

"Now?" Pohatu looked up at the night sky. "But it's getting dark."

"I shall help guide you." Nilkuu said good-bye to Bingzak, then looked at Pohatu and said, "This way."

Nilkuu led Pohatu out of the fortress and they began walking across the desert, heading for a series of dunes to the east. Pohatu quickly fell into step beside Nilkuu and said, "Will you tell me more about this island? And about the other heroes?"

"I shall tell you everything I know," Nilkuu

said. "But keep your eyes peeled for spiders. They're everywhere!"

As they proceeded, Nilkuu wondered if his fellow Protectors had already located the other fallen comets, and if each Toa had arrived without memories.

21

# CHAPTER 2

**"You don't remember**
*anything*?" said Izotor, Protector of Ice, as he discharged his ice blaster at the skull spiders that were crawling through the snow toward him.

"That is quite correct," replied Kopaka, the white-masked Toa, "but I do believe that I know evil when I see it." He swung his ice spear hard to his right, striking three spiders and knocking them straight into a nearby chasm. "I look

23

forward to fighting the fiend that you mentioned, the Lord of Skull Spiders."

"Don't forget what I told you about the Prophecy," Izotor said. "You must first find your Golden Mask at the Shrine of the Mask of Ice." He released another volley of projectiles from his blaster. The projectiles struck the spiders, causing them to freeze instantly. Another spider sprang from a snow bank and angled its sharp legs at Izotor's mask. Izotor saw the incoming spider and responded by activating his ice saw and swinging it upward. The spider sailed headfirst into the saw's rotating blade and landed in two heaps in the snow on either side of Izotor.

Kopaka and Izotor were less than three village-lengths from where Kopaka's comet had smashed into the tundra in Okoto's Region of Ice. Their footprints from the crash site had already vanished under a fresh blanket of falling snow when the spiders attacked. Kopaka turned fast and saw three more spiders scurrying toward him. He reached for the sharp-edged shield that was secured to his back and slammed it into the ice between him and the spiders. The shield's impact sprayed ice shards at the spiders, knocking them onto their backs. Kopaka swung the spear again and sent the spiders into the chasm after the others.

"You are a skilled warrior," Izotor said.

"But I have a feeling our fight has just begun," Kopaka said as he brushed bits of ice from his shield. "Is your island's weather always like this?"

"No, only here in the north. Okoto also has regions of water, jungle, fire, earth, and stone."

"One region for each Protector and Toa?"

"Correct," Izotor said. "Are you certain that you don't remember the names Gali, Lewa, Tahu, Onua, or Pohatu?"

Kopaka nodded. "I'm certain."

Izotor pointed to Kopaka's shield. "According to legend, your frost shield is composed of two pieces. Separate the pieces, attach them to your feet, and they become avalanche skis. You should put them on now."

"Why?"

"So we can leave before those spiders get here."

Kopaka looked around and saw only a white world of snow and ice. "Which spiders? Where?"

Izotor pointed to a distant glacial slope to the east that was barely visible through the falling snow. Kopaka gazed at the slope and said, "I see tiny dark specks on that hill."

"Look again. Closely."

Kopaka tilted his head slightly and was surprised when the dark specks suddenly became larger. He saw hundreds of skull spiders, all marching fast toward his position. He shoved Izotor behind him before he shifted his grip on his own weapons. "There's no time to escape! Stay behind me while I deal with these monsters!"

Izotor cleared his throat. "Actually, the spiders won't get here for several minutes. Your mask has a built-in binocular lens to magnify your vision, so you can better see things that are far away. I guess you forgot about that, too."

"Oh," Kopaka said. He readjusted his vision and the spiders became distant specks again. As he disassembled his shield into two skis, he said, "My memory loss is most frustrating.

Perhaps I am not one of the heroes of your Prophecy. After all, if I'm meant to be the Master of Ice, why am I so cold . . . ?"

Izotor laughed as he stepped around Kopaka so they faced each other. "You only just arrived on Okoto, and you have already defeated many skull spiders. And when you thought we were about to be attacked by more spiders, did you run away or try to hide? No, you did not. You shoved me behind you to protect me, and you prepared to fight. I have no doubt about your courage or your identity. You are a Toa. You are Kopaka. You *are* the Master of Ice. It is your destiny to defeat evil and save the island!"

Kopaka attached the avalanche skis to his feet. "I appreciate your confidence, Izotor."

"Good. But you put on your skis backward."

Kopaka looked down at his skis. "I was just making sure they are durable." He removed his skis, put them on correctly, and then flexed his legs to slide the skis back and forth. "The snow is somewhat slippery. Perhaps I should test these skis on a hill that is not too steep."

"No time for that," said Izotor. Stowing his own weapons, he darted around behind Kopaka and jumped onto Kopaka's back, causing the Toa to bend his knees and launch toward a steep slope. The icy air rushed against Kopaka's white-armored body as he hurtled down the slope with Izotor clinging to his shoulders.

Kopaka said, "We're heading straight for some large rocks."

Izotor leaned hard to his left, which sent Kopaka swerving around a tall frost-covered boulder. Izotor leaned to his right, steering Kopaka through a narrow gap between two outcrops that were covered with thick layers of ice. As they continued down the hill, Izotor said, "Getting the hang of it?"

"I think so," said Kopaka as he veered toward a jagged outcrop. He leaned to his left to avoid the outcrop.

"Look out!" Izotor said before he leaped off Kopaka's back, a split second before Kopaka plowed face first into a high snowbank. Izotor rolled across the snow and came up standing. He looked to the snowbank and saw a deep, hollow impression that was shaped like a silhouette of Kopaka. He was about to call Kopaka's name when the Toa pushed himself out of the snow. Izotor said, "Are you all right?"

"Yes," Kopaka said. "I was just learning how to stop."

"Oh," Izotor said. "You'll catch on soon enough. But perhaps we should walk for a while before you try again."

Kopaka removed his skis and transformed them back into a shield. As he and Izotor proceeded, the falling snow became less dense, allowing them to glimpse mammoth, shadowy structures on the horizon. Using his binocular vision, Kopaka could see windows and other architectural details on various structures. Some windows were open and exposed to the cold, but thick sheets of black ice and daggerlike icicles covered most. Kopaka said, "Is that a city?"

"It *was*," Izotor said. "Like all the great cities in the other regions of Okoto, it is now an ancient tomb. Come. We must walk faster."

The wind howled, churning heavy gusts of snow across the sky, and obscuring Kopaka's view of the ruins. He said, "Did warring armies destroy the cities?"

"No," Izotor said, "not armies, but a clash between just two brothers. The Mask Makers."

# GALI

"Who were the Mask Makers?" said Gali, a Toa clad in blue armor, as she spun her harpoon, whipping it to strike four skull spiders just as they were about to spring at her from a moss-covered rock at the edge of the river.

"Just a moment," said Kivoda, Protector of Water. He aimed his torpedo blaster at an amphibious spider that was swimming toward him. The spider sank under the water. Kivoda saw more spiders coming. He jumped into the river and said, "Master of Water, we must leave immediately or we may soon be overwhelmed."

"Which way do we go?" Gali said as she struck down three more spiders.

"This way." Kivoda powered up the propulsion turbines at his back and dived into the water. Gali kicked out with her foot-mounted shark fins to leave the spiders behind, and dived after Kivoda.

Gali sped swiftly through the water, quickly catching up with Kivoda, who maneuvered his turbines to descend closer to the river's floor. Long shafts of sunlight traveled down from the water's surface, illuminating exotic vegetation and bizarre formations of coral.

Gali glanced back. "I don't see any spiders behind us."

"They're probably already on their way," Kivoda said as he guided Gali past the ruins of an underwater outpost. "Now that the skull spiders have seen you, their master, the Lord of Skull Spiders, must be aware of your presence, too. The spiders will be unrelenting until you find your Golden Mask."

"Which reminds me," Gali said. "You have yet to tell me about the Mask Makers."

"Yes, of course," Kivoda said. "Once, a long time ago, all lived in harmony on Okoto. The island was a fantastic place full of many wonders and beautiful landscapes, a paradise full of great forests, brimming with life. Even then, Protectors served the islanders by protecting them against wild beasts, wildfires, storms, and floods. From the island's elemental forces, two brothers, the Mask Makers, created Masks of Power. Each brother owned a special mask. Ekimu owned the Mask of Creation, and Makuta owned the Mask of Control. Watch out for those fish."

"What? Oh!" Gali saw that she was swimming toward a small school of fish, and she shifted her body to pass by them. "Sorry," she said. "I'm new around here. Please continue, Kivoda."

"The brothers," Kivoda continued, "provided

34

all islanders, including the Protectors, with many masks, but Ekimu's were the most treasured. Makuta became envious and forged an evil plan. Although a sacred law prohibited creating a mask that contained the power of more than one element because such a mask would become too strong and dangerous, Makuta decided to create the most powerful mask of all time. The Mask of Ultimate Power."

"What happened next?"

"When Makuta put on the mask, it took control of him, and the entire island began to shake and crumble. Ekimu realized what Makuta had done, and he managed to knock the mask from his brother's face. This produced an explosion of cataclysmic proportions. Cities crumbled, and a great crater was left at the site of the explosion. A massive shock wave rolled across the land. Most of Okoto's northern part was transformed into a barren wasteland. Earthquakes followed, causing landmasses to shift and volcanoes to erupt. An immense glacier and frozen mountains now dominate the island's northern tip. In the south, three large volcanoes produce thick lava flows. The west is scarred with obsidian plains. Here, in the east, the land became swamps and marshy lakes. Only the southern jungles escaped cataclysm because the mountains protected them. Although thousands of years have passed since the explosion, the effects of Makuta's dark deed are still with us."

Gali said, "What became of the Mask Makers?"

"The shock wave sent both brothers into an endless sleep. It also scattered the Masks of Power all over the island. When the ancient Protectors found the nearly lifeless body of Ekimu, he whispered the Prophecy to them before they laid him to rest. Ever since, many generations of Protectors have made sure that the Masks of Power remained hidden in sacred shrines. And for all those many years, the masks waited for a time when someone would come to find and claim them."

"I don't understand," Gali said. "If you and the other Protectors know that the Masks of Power are hidden in shrines on Okoto, why not claim the masks for yourselves?"

"Because the masks were created for only the strongest, for you and the other Toa. But as we realized that evil was rising and becoming more powerful, we could no longer protect all the villagers, and our need for heroes became more urgent. So my fellow Protectors and I united at the Temple of Time to recite the Prophecy and hastened your arrival."

"Tell me, Kivoda. Did Makuta's spirit survive? Is he responsible for the rising evil?"

"Yes, or so we believe," Kivoda said. "We also believe he controls the Lord of Skull Spiders and countless other monsters."

"I wish I could remember my own past," Gali said, "but I trust your faith in me and the other heroes, and I will do all I can to help your tribes."

"I speak for all the tribes on Okoto when I say we are grateful for your help."

Gali smiled behind her mask. "Is the Shrine of the Mask of Water much farther?"

"We're very close now."

"Then let us swim faster."

As Kivoda guided Gali over the submerged wreckage of an ancient vessel, the waters became unusually warm. Looking down to the river floor, Gali saw something that resembled brightly glowing rocks. Pointing to the area, she said, "What is that?"

"Lava," Kivoda said. "Molten rock. It comes up through thermal vents, which I believe are connected to the volcanoes and lava rivers in the Region of Fire. Keep your distance from lava. It's so hot, it's deadly!"

Gali tried to imagine what a lava river looked like, but she stopped thinking about the Region of Fire as soon as she saw amphibious skull spiders in front of her and Kivoda, blocking the path to the Shrine of the Mask of Water. Kivoda saw the spiders, too, and said, "Remember your destiny."

Gali readied her harpoon. With Kivoda at her side, she swam straight for the spiders.

口凸凶凹石

"Don't these spiders ever let up?" said Tahu, Toa of Fire, who wore a red mask and armor.

"No," said Narmoto, Protector of Fire. "Since your arrival to Okoto, the Lord of Skull Spiders has released even more of his minions to search for the Masks of Power."

Tahu and Narmoto had been traveling up a steep grade of a dark volcanic mountain when dozens of skull spiders attacked. Tahu was armed with two golden swords and also a pair of fire blades that could be combined into a lava-proof surfboard. Narmoto wielded a fire blaster and two flame swords. As their swords slashed at the spiders, Tahu said, "We must reach higher ground."

"This way," said Narmoto. He leaped over several spiders to land on a rocky ledge that jutted out beside a heavy stream of lava. Tahu jumped up after Narmoto, and the vicious spiders turned fast and began crawling up toward the ledge. Without hesitation, Tahu drew his fire blades and held them at an angle against the lava, diverting the flow of molten rock so it fell down upon the spiders. The spiders screeched and tumbled away.

Clouds of smoke billowed up past Tahu. "That smells terrible."

"Keep moving," said Narmoto, who was already scrambling up the steep wall of dark stone. Tahu followed Narmoto up the wall until they arrived at the base of two enormous pillars that appeared to be carved out of the volcano before them. Narmoto said, "This is Okoto's greatest volcano. You are close now."

Looking to the top of the pillars, Tahu saw they supported a high platform that extended to a shadowy doorway. "The shrine is that way?"

"It is."

"How do we get up there?"

"You'll climb."

"What about you?"

Narmoto jumped up onto Tahu's back. "I'm all set," Narmoto said. "Start climbing."

As Tahu began his ascent, he wondered if the other Toa had also reached their destinations, and what dangers awaited within the shrines.

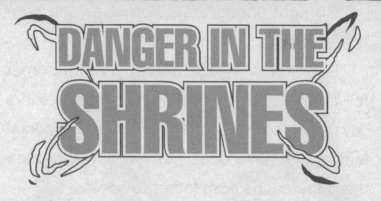

# CHAPTER 3

## DANGER IN THE SHRINES

**"We are very near the** Shrine of the Mask of Earth," said Korgot, Protector of Earth. Korgot was leading Onua, Master of Earth, down rough-hewn steps in a large tunnel, deep below the Region of Earth on the island of Okoto. Bright purple crystals grew from the cave's walls, illuminating the stairway with eerie light. Korgot added, "We might have gotten here faster if we hadn't run into those green skull spiders, the ones that can see in the dark."

Onua said, "May I ask a personal question?"

"Go right ahead," said Korgot as she continued down the steps.

"Back in your village, shortly after my comet fell to Okoto, didn't one of your tribe's elders say that all the Protectors wear sacred Elemental Masks that have been passed down through the generations from father to son?"

"Well, yes. That's how the tradition usually works. But how is that a personal question?"

"Forgive me if I sound ignorant, and please keep in mind that I have no memories before my arrival to your island, but"—Onua cleared his throat—"You are female, aren't you?"

Korgot chuckled. "Yes, I am."

"I thought so," Onua said. "I doubt I would have been so confused if your elders had said that the masks could be passed down to daughters, too."

"Remind me to tell them that," Korgot said as she came to a stop before a wall of solid rock. "The shrine is just beyond this wall." Hoisting her star drill, she said, "I'll use my drill to bore through it."

Onua studied the wall and flexed the turbo shovelers that were clamped over his hands and lower arms. "I think I can reach the other side of this wall faster than your drill."

Korgot lowered her drill. "Be my guest."

Onua dug his massive fingers into the wall and began clawing through the rock, quickly reducing the first layer to rubble. He dug faster, burrowing deeper into the wall, and then swung both arms forward to break through the final layer of stone, making a hole that emptied into another cave. As Onua shoved the rubble aside and stepped through the passage he had created, Korgot said, "Your

47

method of tunneling may be messy, but you get the job done."

Korgot followed Onua into the next cave, which led to a broad ledge that overlooked a deep chasm in an immense underground chamber. The entire chamber was lined with giant, glowing crystals, and one towering crystal, a natural obelisk that grew up from the floor. Onua and Korgot saw a single golden mask hovering in the air directly above the top of the tower.

Korgot said, "You must scale that tower to obtain your mask and fulfill your destiny. I'll remain here and watch for skull spiders."

Onua left the ledge and scampered down to the chamber's floor, taking care not to break any of the glowing crystals. As soon as he arrived at the base of the crystal obelisk, he began climbing up, moving hand over hand until he reached the top. Pulling himself up to stand on the obelisk, he glanced back to the ledge where Korgot stood, watching him. Onua saw that Korgot wasn't alone on the ledge.

Dozens of green skull spiders had snuck up through the corridor behind Korgot. Korgot raised her star drill and also drew one of her throwing knives. From where Onua stood, he could see that the Protector was greatly outnumbered, and that she had nowhere to run.

Korgot shouted, "It's too late for me, Onua. Fulfill the Prophecy!"

Onua removed his own mask as he reached for the Golden Mask of Power, and slapped the Golden Mask over his face. He was almost overwhelmed by the incredible surge of power that came with donning the Golden Mask. Moving faster than thought, he instinctively transformed his turbo shovelers into a broad-headed hammer and leaped from the obelisk, vaulting over the chasm to land on the ledge beside Korgot.

The green skull spiders were about to pounce on Korgot when Onua swung his hammer, bringing it down hard upon the ledge. Charged with elemental power, the hammer's impact blasted the spiders, smashing their bodies against the cavern's walls.

Korgot gasped. "You created the earthquake hammer, just as the legends foretold!"

But Onua didn't hear Korgot. He only heard a strange voice that seemed to be speaking from within his own head.

And the voice was calling his name.

# ᕼᓂᒍᔕᕼᕮ

"Listen, Lewa," whispered Vizuna, Protector of Jungle, as he adjusted his grip on his flame bow.

Lewa, Toa of Jungle, cocked his green-masked head to the side and said, "Except for those bright bugs flying around my golden mask, I don't hear anything."

"Exactly," Vizuna said. "It's *too* quiet."

After cutting through thick woodlands and fighting numerous skull spiders, Lewa and Vizuna had finally arrived at the ruins of the Shrine of the Mask of Jungle. Enormous trees bordered the ruins, and the central area was filled with bizarre, luminescent roots that snaked around a tall dais. The Golden Mask of the Jungle hovered above the dais, which was surrounded by glowing, buzzing fireflies that were apparently attracted to the mask's power. It almost appeared as if the strange life inside the ruins emanated from the Golden Mask itself.

Looking around, Vizuna said, "I sense this shrine is filled with many dangers."

"Oh?" said Lewa. "Is that your brain talking, or your tail?"

Vizuna groaned. Shortly after Lewa had arrived on Okoto, the Toa had inquired about the green articulated tail that was attached to the base of Vizuna's lower spine. Vizuna had explained that the tail was equipped with built-in sensors that detected environmental fluctuations and enabled him to find water and predict the weather, but Lewa simply found the tail amusing.

"Joke about my tail all you want," Vizuna said. "It has served me well in the war against the skull spiders."

A loud snap came from behind Lewa. He drew both his swords as he spun fast at the waist and brought the swords down quickly through a cluster of broad green leaves. Lewa's swords crashed against the back of a large blue skull spider that had been skulking across the jungle floor. The spider stopped moving.

"I told you I sensed danger," said Vizuna.

"I wish you'd sensed it a little sooner," Lewa said as he pulled his swords free. He heard more snapping sounds throughout the ruins. "Sounds like this critter brought all his pals along."

Readying his bow, Vizuna said, "Go for your mask, Lewa. I'll hold off the spiders!"

Lewa possessed an X-glider that allowed him to fly. He was about to take flight toward the Golden Mask when he saw hordes of spiders creeping toward the central dais, and also descending from the vines and branches that loomed over the hovering mask. Determined to evade the spiders, he leaped onto a massive, thorn-covered green root that encircled the dais, and let his momentum carry him across its surface.

Surfing the root as if it were a fixed wave, Lewa neatly dodged the spiny thorns as he swept toward his goal. Snatching the Golden Mask, he transferred it over his face and instantly felt its elemental power flow through him. He was still moving across the vine when he saw Vizuna was completely surrounded by spiders.

Lewa leaped from the root and flew toward his ally. Moving his swords against the mystical flight blades that composed his X-glider, he transformed the swords into a pair of battle-axes. The axes glowed with energy as he raised them. He bellowed, "I am the Master of Jungle!"

The spiders blew away from Vizuna as if they had been struck by a hurricane. As the spiders crashed and clattered against the shrine's ancient trees, Lewa was surprised to hear a strange voice calling his name. He was even more surprised when he saw, in his mind, the sprawling ruins of an ancient city.

# TASU

Pohatu, Toa of Stone, saw the spiders swarming toward Nilkuu, Protector of Stone, and was about to run to help his ally when Nilkuu shouted, "Forget about me, Pohatu! Fulfill your destiny while you can!"

They were at the bottom of a deep, long trench—all that remained of the Shrine of the Mask of Stone, which had been buried beneath the sand for many centuries. The trench ended against a high wall, where a pair of ancient stone statues of warriors stood on either side of a tall, carved-stone pillar, above which hovered a Golden Mask of Power. After having spent weeks fighting their way across desert dunes, they had finally arrived at the ruins just as an army of skull spiders also discovered the shrine.

As the invading spiders drew closer to Nilkuu, Pohatu made his move. Generating a tornado, he ascended up through the trench and seized the Golden Mask. Still soaring above the trench, he quickly removed his original mask and replaced it with the Golden Mask. He felt the Golden Mask's power flow through his body.

Pohatu landed on the trench floor and drew his stormerangs. He whipped both stormerangs at the same time, sending them spinning over the spiders that had backed Nilkuu against a wall. The power of the Golden Mask combined with the stormerangs to produce a sandstorm with explosive force, and the sudden burst of wind and sand hurled the spiders away in all directions.

Nilkuu gazed in awe as the spinning stormerangs sailed back to Pohatu's waiting hands. After Pohatu caught the weapons, he turned to Nilkuu and said, "Are you all right?"

Nilkuu nodded. "And yourself?"

Pohatu extended his arms and flexed his fingers. "The Golden Mask has filled me with incredible power. I feel as if I could take on the . . . the . . . that's strange." He rocked back on his feet and held his hands up over the sides of his mask. "I can hear someone. Someone calling my name."

"The voice comes from within your mask," Nilkuu said. "It is the voice of Ekimu, the Mask Maker."

Nilkuu had told Pohatu about the two brothers, Ekimu and Makuta, and how their masks had shaped not only the history but the geography of the island. Pohatu said, "The mask makes me *see* something, too. I see . . . a magnificent city! It's surrounded by clouds and mountains. And a long, stone footbridge appears to be the city's gateway."

"You see the city of the Mask Makers, where Ekimu is entombed. The city is in the southeast, in the Jungle Region."

Pohatu gasped as the Golden Mask presented a sharper vision of the city. "All the buildings are in ruins. Something terrible must have happened there a long time ago. And I sense that something even more terrible is waiting there now."

"The evil is growing stronger," Nilkuu said, "and the Lord of Skull Spiders gains more power every day."

"Then we must go to the city at once!"

Nilkuu shook his head. "Not *us*, Master of Stone. *You* must go there. Obtaining your Golden Mask was but your first step. The true quest is ahead of you. And where you must go, the other Protectors and I cannot follow."

"You mean, I am to find the Mask Maker and confront the evil alone?"

"No, Toa Pohatu. On this quest, all six heroes shall unite."

Pohatu and Nilkuu walked past motionless skull spiders and exited the shrine. Nilkuu pointed to a distant mountain range and said, "Go that way. The Golden Mask will guide you to the city of the Mask Maker."

Pohatu bowed to Nilkuu. "You are a brave warrior, Protector of Stone. It was an honor to fight by your side."

Nilkuu bowed in return. "The honor was mine, Master of Stone. Now hurry to the city!"

Pohatu took several long strides away from Nilkuu before he generated a tornado that lifted him high over the desert and carried him toward the mountains. And while Pohatu traveled across the sky, he thought about the other heroes. He wondered if they had also obtained their Golden Masks and were now making their way to the city of the Mask Maker. He also wondered if all the heroes were fully prepared to fight whatever evil waited for them.

He imagined he would soon find out.

# CHAPTER 4

## THE MYSTERIOUS CITY

**High in the mountains**
in the Region of Jungle, at the very edge of a
cliff, a majestic gateway with intricately carved
details served as the entrance to a long, monumental bridge that was the primary access
to the city of the Mask Maker. The bridge
spanned a deep chasm, and despite the
bridge's obvious age, the sharp edges of its
towers had not dulled over time. The bridge's
foundation vanished into a river of clouds that
flowed through the chasm, and the clouds

created the illusion that the city was floating in the sky.

Green jungle growth had consumed most of the city, covering nearly every surface. The gateway and bridge were also adorned with incredibly large spider webs, made by the skull spiders to scare off or snare trespassers. At the center of the bridge, spider-spun cocoons, holding the spiders' victims, dangled below an octagonal observation deck.

Onua, Gali, Kopaka, Lewa, and Pohatu arrived at the gateway at the same time. All were wearing their Golden Masks. They gazed at one another skeptically, unsure about what to say to one another, when Tahu, carrying his surfboard and also wearing a Golden Mask, emerged from behind the gateway.

"Greetings! I am Tahu, Master of Fire. The prophecy has brought us together under my command."

"Your command?" said Kopaka as he shifted his grip on his frost shield. "Did your brain catch fire? I am Kopaka, and I work under no command!"

Tahu and Kopaka glared at each other. Hoping to break the tension, Onua said politely, "I am Onua, Master of Earth." Pohatu, Gali, and Lewa quickly identified themselves.

Ignoring the others, Tahu and Kopaka snarled simultaneously, threw down their weapons, and charged each other. Fists clanged against armor as they fought in the gateway's shadow. Grappling in their heavy armor, they toppled to the ground, and continued wrestling as Gali stepped up beside them, jabbed her harpoon between their bodies, and said, "Stop it, you idiots!"

Tahu and Kopaka didn't listen. They kept hammering away until Onua leaned over and grabbed their heads with his massive hands.

Onua lifted them up until their feet dangled beneath them, then shifted his hands to force Tahu and Kopaka to face each other. Onua let out a good-natured laugh before he said, "Don't fight."

In Onua's grasp, Kopaka and Tahu looked like helpless puppets, but they continued to exchange menacing glares until Tahu said, "We still need a leader."

Gali said, "We'll have a vote, then."

"I vote for Onua," said Lewa. "He knows how to *grab* attention." Lewa chuckled loudly.

"Quiet," said Pohatu as he looked toward the bridge. "We've got company."

The other heroes followed Pohatu's gaze. Onua was still holding Tahu and Kopaka, and he adjusted his grip so that they also faced the bridge. All were astonished to see something that resembled long, articulated black spears rising up over the edge of the bridge's central observation deck. A cloud billowed across the bridge, temporarily obscuring the heroes' view.

Onua released Tahu and Kopaka. Keeping his eyes fixed on the bridge, Tahu said, "What is that thing?"

And then the cloud cleared, revealing that the black spears were actually the six legs of an enormous monster with an armored exoskeleton. The monster's wide, black head had four fiery red eyes that were set over broad, powerful jaws. Shifting on its sharply tapered legs, the monster opened its jaws to expose sharp white teeth, and released a hiss so powerful that the heroes could smell its wretched breath across the distance.

"The Lord of Skull Spiders," said Pohatu. "We can't outrun him." Pohatu drew his stormerangs and readied himself for battle.

"Don't worry," Kopaka said as he raised

his own weapons. "I can freeze this bug all on my own!"

Lewa snickered. "You're too slow, Kopaka." And then Kopaka launched away from the group, tearing through the gateway and onto the bridge, sprinting straight for the Lord of Skull Spiders.

Gali raced up behind Lewa, shoved him aside with her harpoon, and said, "I'll flush it away!"

Seeing Gali's approach, the monster spat hard, releasing a gob of its sticky web fluid. The gob struck Gali, instantly coating her with webbing that pinned her arms and legs. She stumbled and collapsed onto the bridge. As she wriggled to free herself from the webbing, she saw Onua, Kopaka, and Tahu run past her, each determined to be first to attack the monster.

Pohatu generated a tornado and blasted past the others, knocking them aside, and nearly sending Tahu off the bridge. Moving fast toward the Lord of Skull Spiders, Pohatu drew a stormerang and flung it at the monster. The monster responded by flicking up one leg, which struck the stormerang and knocked it into the sky, and then spat another gob of web fluid.

The gob struck Pohatu's head with so much force that it lifted him up and out of his own tornado, launching him backward in a high arc above the bridge. As his tornado rapidly vanished, he crashed down on top of a very surprised Kopaka. A moment later, Pohatu's stormerang returned to him, striking him hard against the side of his Golden Mask.

"Make way for the Master of Fire!" Tahu said as he bounded past Pohatu and Kopaka with his fire blades held out before him. As he neared the Lord of Skull Spiders, the monster raised its two front legs to block his attack.

The fireblades clanged loudly against the monster's armored legs. Tahu struck again and again, but his blows had no apparent effect. He was not prepared when the monster flicked its front legs hard, flinging him into the air in the same arcing trajectory as Pohatu had left the monster. As Tahu felt gravity tug him back toward the bridge, he braced himself for a rough landing. To his relief, he landed not on the bridge but in Onua's outstretched arms.

Tahu saw the other heroes were on their feet, and that both Gali and Pohatu had removed the webbing from their bodies. He looked up at Onua. Onua said, "We must work *together*."

The other heroes nodded in silent agreement. Onua lowered Tahu to stand beside him, and they all faced the Lord of Skull Spiders. The monster gazed back in defiance and hissed again.

As the heroes readied their weapons, they felt their elemental powers building within them. The six heroes sprang forward, moving as one toward their enemy. Although they had never fought as a team before, they moved like a veteran tactical group.

The Lord of Skull Spiders spat an ugly gob at the approaching heroes. Kopaka caught the gob on his frost shield and kept running. Lewa took to the air at the same moment that Pohatu ascended by tornado.

The monster's four eyes were unable to keep track of each hero. Gali's harpoon struck the monster first, followed by Lewa's battle-axes. The combined assault knocked the monster off its feet, and its head crashed against the bridge with a sickening thud. Before the monster could rise, Pohatu whipped a stormerang that smashed into the monster's head, at the central point between all four eyes.

Tahu channeled his power into a punch that sent the monster flying into the air. The monster came crashing down on the far side of the observation deck, landing on its back. Tahu shouted, "Onua! Now!"

Onua swung his earthquake hammer and brought it down directly in front of his feet, smashing the observation deck's stone surface. The impact created a massive crack that traveled across the deck and around the monster, and then the entire broken chunk of stone beneath the monster dislodged from the bridge. The chunk fell away into the clouds below, taking the Lord of Skull Spiders with it.

Pohatu's stormerang returned to him and he plucked it from the air. The six heroes stepped up to the edge of the broken area of the deck and peered down at the clouds. Gali said, "We did it! United, the masks hold the power to defeat evil!"

"I *knew* we could work together," said Onua.

"And by defeating the Lord of Skull Spiders," said Pohatu, "we've released all the islanders who were under his control!"

Lewa said, "I don't mean to sound like a spoilsport, but despite our victory here, does anyone else still sense evil in the air?"

"I do," said Kopaka.

"We all feel it," said Tahu. "It seems our senses are also united by the Golden Masks."

Pohatu noticed a cylindrical podium on the

observation deck. "I wonder what used to be here."

"*Shh!* Quiet," said Tahu. "I have that weird voice in my head again."

The other heroes heard the voice, too. Sounding very old and weary, the voice said, "I am Ekimu the Mask Maker. You have all shown great courage. You are true heroes. But now you must hurry, and find my resting place."

A vision came to all the heroes through their masks. They saw the interior of a shadowy tomb that held a golden coffin, and the coffin was decorated with symbols that represented Ekimu.

The vision vanished. The heroes gazed down the length of the bridge to the cloud-shrouded city that awaited them. Lewa leaped to the sky and glided over the group, watching for any sign of danger as they proceeded across the bridge.

They arrived at a street made of interlocked octagonal stone tiles that led into the city's outskirts. The once-smooth path had become overgrown with weeds and trees. The surrounding buildings were mostly pyramidal ziggurats, rectangular towers with sloped sides, and flat terraces that could be reached by open stairways.

Flying overhead, Lewa saw many moss-covered ruins but not a single skull spider. Because green plants and massive thorny vines covered nearly every structure, it was difficult to distinguish one building from the next, and Lewa imagined it would be easy for his allies to get lost. He spied several stone statues and clusters of obelisks that made him realize he was flying over an expansive graveyard.

He watched the other heroes enter the graveyard. Bordered by a high wall, the graveyard contained many tombstones and burial chambers, and its stone-tile paths were over-run with roots and vines. As Lewa descended to rejoin the group, he heard Gali say, "We need to find Ekimu before the forces of evil."

Lewa touched down on top of a stone obelisk. "Finding anything in this mess is harder than finding a needle in a hay stack."

"The *masks* will guide us," said Onua, sounding jovial and remarkably unconcerned.

Pohatu surveyed the jungly graveyard. "I don't like this place. Something evil is hiding here."

Lewa jumped down from the obelisk. The six heroes pressed on, staying on the stone-tile path as they entered an enclosed courtyard filled with rubble. The path extended to an open gateway. None of the heroes heard the sound of breaking stone tiles from behind, or saw the skeletal metal hand that had thrust itself up through the tiles from underground.

"Careful," said Pohatu. "I smell a trap."

The heroes were only halfway across the courtyard when Tahu stepped on a loose tile, accidentally triggering an ancient hidden mechanism. At the far end of the courtyard, the gateway's doors suddenly slammed shut, and an intricate array of locking mechanisms clacked across the doors, sealing them tight. Instead of admitting responsibility, Tahu said, "No problem. I'll think up a plan."

"That would take forever," Kopaka said testily. "Follow *my* lead instead."

Tahu's eyes blazed with rage. Scowling behind his mask, he let out a low, angry snarl as he took a threatening step toward Kopaka. Onua moved fast to position himself between the Master of Ice and the Master of Fire. Onua said, "*United*, remember?"

Pohatu gestured for the others to lower their voices. "You're loud enough to wake the dead."

"Pohatu's right," Gali said. "Be quiet. We don't know what's behind that gate."

"Ask nicely," Lewa said, "and I might tell you." He sprang and soared up over the area to get a better view.

Lewa was still ascending when a sharp-tipped arrow whizzed past Tahu. He raised his surfboard, holding it up like a shield, and said, "We're under fire!"

"I hate fire," said Kopaka as he held up his own shield.

More arrows rained down from the sky. Dodging and ducking the projectiles, Onua, Gali, and Pohatu quickly took cover behind Kopaka and Tahu. They looked to the roof above the inner gateway and saw a group of metal-boned skeleton archers. The skeletons immediately released another volley of arrows.

Kopaka activated the elemental energy in his frost shield, which projected an energy sphere over him and his allies. As dozens of arrows pinged and shattered against the shield, Gali glanced back across the court-yard, searching for an escape route.

Gali saw more skeleton archers moving behind the heroes' position. Some skeletons pushed their way up through the ground. Others lurched out from the rubble in the courtyard. Gali said, "Bury them, Onua! They're blocking the way out!"

Kopaka deactivated his frost shield, let-ting the energy sphere vanish and allowing Onua to move freely. Onua raised his earth-quake hammer and slammed it down into the ground in front of the approaching skeletons. The impact created a huge crack across the courtyard, jolting the ancient structures and knocking the skeletons off their feet. The crack rapidly expanded into a deep crevice and the skeletons tumbled into it.

The effect of Onua's hammer didn't stop at the far end of the courtyard. The earthquake continued its violent journey all the way to the bridge that had delivered the heroes to the city of the Mask Makers. From where the heroes stood, they could see the bridge's towers crumble and collapse.

"There's no way out," Pohatu said.

The skeleton archers above the gateway resumed shooting arrows at the heroes. Tahu raised his surfboard for protection again, and said, "Toa! Stand united!"

As Kopaka shifted his own shield to deflect more arrows, he said, "Where is Lewa?"

And then they saw Lewa, diving down from the sky. He extended his arms as he swooped fast behind the skeletons, using his arms to knock them from their perch. As the skeletons fell into the courtyard, the other heroes energized their weapons and swept forward. Lewa landed in the courtyard and watched as his allies made quick work of the skeletons, reducing the archers to scattered piles of bones.

After all the archers were destroyed, Kopaka said, "What took you so long, Lewa?"

"I spotted an arena," Lewa said casually. "It could be fun."

Kopaka glowered. "We're not looking for fun. We're looking for Ekimu!"

Gali studied the gateway's closed doors and said, "We need to get past the gate first."

Pohatu walked over to a giant boulder that lay amidst the rubble beside the crevice he'd created. Using both hands, he lifted the boulder over his head and hurled it at the doors. The boulder crashed through the doors, sending them flying into the alley that lay beyond.

Gali, Onua, and Tahu looked at Pohatu with admiration. Lewa looked at Kopaka and said, "So. What about the arena?"

"We're *not* going to the arena," said Kopaka. "Follow me."

"I go where I want, freeze-brain," Lewa said.

Ignoring Lewa's remark, Kopaka and the other Toa started walking for the open gateway, leaving Lewa behind. The Master of Jungle scoffed before he leaped into the air. Rising over the city, he angled off to the area where he'd seen the arena.

It was a decision Lewa would soon regret.

# CHAPTER 5

**SKULL SLICER STRIKES**

**Lewa landed in a court-** yard outside the arena that he'd spotted from his earlier aerial survey of the city of the Mask Makers. The courtyard was decorated with statues and monuments that were dedicated to long-dead heroes, athletes, and warriors.

Walking up to a wall that was covered with vines, Lewa pushed aside the vines to reveal carved reliefs that illustrated the rules for ancient games. From what he could decipher, one game in particular could be played by only the strongest and the bravest islanders. He leaned forward so he could examine the illustrations more closely. From what he could see, the game required competitors to jump across hexagonal pedestals that rose and fell through holes in an arena floor. The pedestals appeared to operate by levers made out of stone.

Without warning, the wall before him exploded outward and a clawed skeletal hand launched out, grabbed Lewa's mask, and snatched it from his face. Lewa collapsed unconscious to the arena floor.

# POHATU

Kopaka led Pohatu, Tahu, Gali, and Onua down an alley that ended with a closed door. Pohatu said, "This is the wrong way."

"No," Kopaka said indignantly as he pushed the door open. "The wrong way was the one taken by—" The Master of Ice's words caught in his throat. He saw that the doorway opened directly into a courtyard outside an arena, and he realized he'd accidentally led his allies directly to the place he'd intended to avoid.

"Lewa?!" said Gali, who was first to see Lewa's body lying beside some rocky rubble at the base of a wall that had a freshly punched hole in it.

As the heroes ran to their fallen friend, they heard terrible laughter that echoed down from the top of a nearby stairway. They looked to the stairway and saw who was laughing. He was a fearsome skeletal creature wearing a highly stylized skull mask. Two arms extended from each side of his body, and three long

87

swords were secured to his back. In his upper right hand, the creature held Lewa's Golden Mask. He ran off, vanishing into a shadowy doorway.

Pohatu picked up Lewa and saw the Master of Jungle's eyes flicker open. "Lewa! What happened?"

"I was looking at that wall," Lewa muttered weakly as he gestured to the wall with the hole in it. "I was looking at the rules . . . for an ancient game when that creature with four arms stole my mask. He calls himself . . . Skull Slicer."

Kopaka said, "Come. We must go after him and recover Lewa's mask."

Ascending the stairway to follow Skull Slicer, Pohatu carried Lewa while their allies stayed close beside them, protecting Lewa in his defenseless state. Moving through the shadowy doorway, they proceeded into the arena.

The arena had high walls and a floor that was riddled with shifting tiles, height-adjustable columns, and large cantilevers that extended and retracted into the walls. Seeing their quarry, Kopaka pointed to one column and said, "There!"

Skull Slicer stood atop the column. He removed his stylized skull mask and rapidly replaced it with Lewa's Golden Mask of Power.

Lewa went limp in Pohatu's arms. Kopaka said, "What's happening?"

"There's a special link between master and mask," Pohatu said.

Looking at Skull Slicer, Gali said, "So that thing is stealing Lewa's energy?"

Throughout the arena, floor tiles began spinning and columns shifted their heights and positions. A wide cylindrical vent released a burst of fire behind Skull Slicer, but as the skeletal warrior began glowing with elemental energy, he just laughed, ignored the flames, and leaped to the top of another column.

Lewa appeared to grow even weaker. Gali surveyed the arena, tried desperately to make sense out of the moving tiles and columns, and then cried, "Lewa! You read the rules. What do we do?"

Lewa mumbled incoherently. Onua said, "He is too weak."

Struggling to get words out, Lewa whispered, "Hit . . . the . . . lever . . ."

Gali was unable to hear Lewa over the noise of the surrounding mechanisms. Leaning close to Pohatu, she asked, "What is he saying?"

"The *lever*," Pohatu said as he handed Lewa's body to Gali. "Onua! Go bash!"

To reach the lever, Onua saw that he needed to run between two of the large beams that were pumping in and out of the arena through slots in the walls. He ran as fast as he could, but as he began to pass between the beams, he realized they were about to strike from both sides. He closed his eyes as he braced for the impact, and was surprised when it didn't happen. Opening his eyes, he looked up and saw Kopaka had jumped up above him, and had braced his legs against the two beams, preventing them from striking Onua.

"You're welcome," said Kopaka.

Skull Slicer looked at Pohatu, who jumped down to the base of a wall and flung his stormerangs at the mask-stealing fiend. The stormerangs struck Skull Slicer's lower arms, pinning them to the wall behind him. With his upper left arm, Skull Slicer unleashed a whip that was tipped with a mask-grabbing claw.

The claw went straight for Kopaka, but he elevated his shield, and managed to block the hook before he yanked the whip from Skull Slicer's hand.

Tahu charged Skull Slicer and knocked a sword from the villain's grip, but Skull Slicer moved fast, grabbing him and holding him tight against his skeletal body.

"Tahu!" Kopaka shouted as he advanced to attack. "You're in my way!" He threw a punch and Tahu ducked, allowing Kopaka's fist to travel straight into Skull Slicer's head. Lewa's mask fell from Skull Slicer's face, Tahu was freed, and Skull Slicer's body slumped forward with his lower arms still pinned to the wall. Kopaka quickly picked up Lewa's mask.

Onua charged. Carrying his earthquake hammer, he leaped and landed on top of Skull Slicer, using the villain as a stepping-stone to jump higher. Onua brought his hammer down on a lever at the top of a high column, which triggered the arena floor to shift, revealing deep, open pits. Skull Slicer lost his balance and fell down into one of the deeper pits.

The heroes quickly regrouped on the arena floor and gathered around Lewa. Kopaka put the recovered Golden Mask onto Lewa's face, and Lewa said, "What happened?"

"I hit the lever," Onua said proudly.

Lewa said, "Without breaking anything?"

Before Onua could answer, the lever that he'd struck with his hammer fell away from the top of the column. The heroes saw cracks rapidly travel through the column, and the arena floor began quaking.

And then the entire arena collapsed, and drove the six heroes down through the floor.

Pinned under a boulder and what felt like a mountain of rubble, Lewa said, "Without breaking anything, huh?"

Onua frowned. All six heroes were similarly stuck under large, heavy stones. Gali said, "We're trapped."

"This is ridiculous," said Pohatu. "I didn't sign up for this mission!"

"None of us did," said Tahu with a sigh. Sounding slightly dazed, he continued, "We just seemed to fall from the stars. Not knowing our purpose. The villagers were in danger."

Gali said, "Skull spiders everywhere."

"Under evil Makuta's control," said Pohatu.

"Even underground," said Onua.

Tahu said, "The Protectors would just keep on fighting for us, to get the Golden Masks."

"They gave us purpose," said Onua.

Kopaka said, "It's our duty to save Okoto."

"I agree," said Pohatu as he tried to wriggle his limbs from under the stones. "But we're still stuck."

"Wait," said Lewa. "I feel a breeze. There must be a tunnel behind these rocks."

"Breeze?!" Kopaka said. "What are you? The Master of *Air*?"

Onua put one hand onto a rock and said, "Lewa's right. Stand back!"

Onua began charging with elemental energy. Seeing him glowing, Gali gasped, "How?"

The surrounding stones exploded. The blast carried the heroes up, launching them through dirt and dust until they spilled out of a hole at the surface. Looking around, they saw the blast had delivered them to a sprawling graveyard. Kopaka said, "Look for Ekimu's tomb." Gali looked at a cluster of ancient tombstones and said, "I don't feel like asking the neighbors for directions."

Lewa, his powers nearly revived, jumped on top of a tombstone. Pointing to a large mausoleum that overlooked the graveyard, he said, "We *could* just take a peek in the building with the huge Mask Maker sign."

The others looked at the mausoleum. A long flight of steps led up to the building's massive doorway, above which rested a monumental stone sculpture of Ekimu's mask. "Let's go," said Tahu. "No stopping us now."

They started walking but before they could reach the mausoleum's steps, the ground began shaking violently. Glancing back across the graveyard, the heroes saw two gigantic Skull Scorpios emerge from the shadows. Each Skull Scorpio wore a silver skull mask and had red eyes. They had two arms with lobster-like claws, walked on six legs, and had long, jointed tails that curved up over their backs. The tails were tipped with articulated poisonous stingers. Pohatu had encountered the monsters during his journey across the Region of Stone, and he muttered, "I hate Scorpios."

"Beware of their stinger tails," said Onua, who had also fought the creatures in the Region of Earth. But before the mighty Master of Earth could raise his earthquake hammer, he watched helplessly as one Skull Scorpio whipped its tail straight for Pohatu's head and snatched his mask.

Pohatu collapsed. Kopaka leaped to Pohatu's side and activated his frost shield to protect his fallen ally in a sphere of energy while Gali and Tahu powered up their own weapons and charged at the Skull Scorpios. The monsters flicked their massive tails and sent both Gali and Tahu crashing into nearby tombstones.

The Skull Scorpios went after Lewa, who leaped from one tombstone to another to avoid the monsters as their deadly tails smashed the stones. Grazed by a chunk of flying rubble, the still-weakened Lewa tried to fly away but veered off course toward the mausoleum, and smacked against a ledge above the mausoleum's doors.

Lewa pulled himself up onto the ledge and stood beside the stone sculpture of Ekimu's mask. Turning fast, he saw the Skull Scorpios skittering up the steps, just below his position. One Skull Scorpio was carrying Pohatu's mask.

Kopaka was still protecting Pohatu when he saw the Skull Scorpios racing up the mausoleum's stairway. Lifting his gaze, he was outraged to see Lewa ducking behind the sculpture of Ekimu's mask. He said, "Stay and fight, coward!"

The sound of breaking stone came from Lewa's position, and Kopaka saw a large crack appear on the sculpture's visage, splitting the monumental mask in half. The two pieces fell away from the ledge, revealing Lewa behind the sculpture's base, holding his battle-axe, which he'd used to shatter the sculpture. The last things that the startled Skull Scorpios saw were the broken pieces of the sculpture, which crashed down upon the monsters, smothering them. The Skull Scorpio that had stolen Pohatu's Golden Mask reflexively opened its claws and released the mask, which landed before the doorway.

Lewa leaped down and picked up Pohatu's mask.

Impressed, Kopaka grudgingly admitted, "That was solid work, Lewa."

Lewa placed the Golden Mask back on Pohatu's face, and Pohatu revived immediately. The six heroes faced the mausoleum's doors. Pohatu said, "Time to meet the Mask Maker."

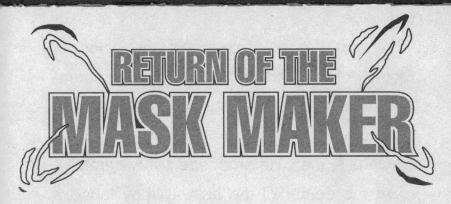

# CHAPTER 6

# RETURN OF THE MASK MAKER

## The doors to Ekimu's

mausoleum opened with a loud creak. Daylight illuminated the tomb's grand hallway for the first time in ages as the heroes entered. The hall was lined with colossal pillars and tall pedestals, which supported sculptures, large vases, and other ancient relics. The walls bore carved reliefs that illustrated events of the Mask Maker's life and accomplishments, and a mural on the ceiling displayed symbols related to Okoto's six regions.

*"You are close,"* said an aged, disembodied voice.

All the heroes recognized the voice of Ekimu. As they moved deeper into the chamber, Lewa said, "Okay. Let's not break anything in here."

Onua sighed. He proceeded very carefully.

At the center of the hallway they found a large, ornately designed sarcophagus. As they walked toward it, they heard Ekimu's weary voice rasp, *"When times are dark, and all hope seems lost, evoke the power of past and future."*

The heroes pushed at the sarcophagus's lid and it slid back. Inside the sarcophagus, Ekimu lay motionless with his hands draped across his chest. His small body was clad in armor that looked thin, brittle, and extremely old. Behind his mask, his eyes were closed. Although the heroes had never seen him before, all of them felt as if they carried clear memories of Ekimu.

"Now what?" said Pohatu.

At the same moment, the heroes remembered a line from the Prophecy of Heroes.

*United, the elements hold the power.*

Acting on instinct, the heroes extended their hands in front of the sarcophagus. Elemental energy began to spark and flow. A giant flash of light erupted from within the sarcophagus, temporarily blinding the heroes. When the light dissipated, they saw the elderly Ekimu standing in his sarcophagus. Behind his mask, his eyes were open. The heroes knelt and bowed their heads to Ekimu.

"Brave Toa," Ekimu said, sounding aged and weary. "You are . . . You are *late!*"

Surprised, the heroes looked at each other for a moment before Kopaka boldly returned his gaze to Ekimu and said, "If you had called an army of real warriors like me, this would have taken no time."

"Your power comes not from numbers," Ekimu said patiently as he stretched his legs. "Your power comes from *unity*. But duty awaits. We must hurry."

Ekimu jumped out of the sarcophagus and almost collapsed because his joints were so old and rusty. Onua grabbed Ekimu's hand and helped him to stand upright. As Ekimu rose, he glimpsed the tomb's open doorway. Despite his ancient joints, he shuffled fast to the doorway so he could see outside.

Ekimu squinted at the bright sunlight. Surveying the once great city, he saw smoke rising from the ruins and gasped. "Evil has destroyed so much."

"Actually," Onua said, "some of it is—"

106

Lewa clapped one hand over Onua's mouth to stop Onua from admitting that he'd destroyed a number of structures since his arrival in the city. "So, Ekimu," Lewa said. "You spoke of duty. What is happening?" Still facing the ruins, Ekimu replied, "He took it just before you arrived."

Gali said, "Who took what?"

"They call him Skull Grinder," Ekimu said. "He is under my brother, Makuta's control. The Mask of Creation. *My* mask. He is on his way to destroy it. If he succeeds, all is lost."

Gali said, "You're saying that Makuta has risen, too? That your brother is responsible for the rising evil on Okoto?"

"I don't know that he has risen *physically*, as I have," Ekimu said, "but his evil has definitely survived and now manipulates others to accomplish his dark goals."

Pohatu said, "Where would Skull Grinder go to destroy a mask?"

"There is only one place," Ekimu said. "My forge." He looked to a nearby hilltop, on which stood an unusual, angular tower. The tower had a flat roof, and the upper side of one wall jutted out, making the entire building resemble an enormous anvil.

Ekimu ran away from the tomb as fast as his aged legs could carry him. He shuffled through the ruins, heading up the hill to the anvil-like tower. As the heroes ran after him, he said, "Watch out for Skull Grinder's servant, Skull Basher. He could be anywhere!"

Lewa said, "What does he look like?"

"Very tall. And wide. And he has big, sharp horns."

When they neared the tower, they saw its upper windows light up. The light cast an ominous shadow of Skull Grinder against the windowpanes. Ekimu said, "He has started my furnace!"

"Let *me* cool things down," Kopaka said.

"Hey!" said Tahu, stepping beside Kopaka. "Fire is *my* element!"

Forgetting about the need for unity, Kopaka and Tahu sprinted up a staircase that led to the tower's entrance, an open doorway that was bracketed by two broad columns. They ran alongside each other, and each was determined to be the first one into the tower. When they reached the doorway, their shoulders collided and both became stuck between the columns.

Skull Basher, a hulking figure with two long horns that extended from his head, was waiting inside the doorway. In each of his massive hands, he wielded a giant hook axe. Before Kopaka and Tahu could attempt to extract themselves, Skull Basher swung his powerful arms out at their bodies, knocking them out of the doorway and into the air. Kopaka and Tahu sailed over the heads of their allies and crashed to the ground behind Onua.

Onua leaped forward and ran up the staircase, ready to use his earthquake hammer against Skull Basher. He was just about to strike when Skull Basher quickly dipped his own head down, lowering his horns so that one horn's sharp tip caught against the bottom of Onua's mask. Skull Basher flung his head back, launching Onua backward and off his feet. Onua bounced down the staircase and rolled to a stop at the feet of his allies. When the other heroes and Ekimu looked back up at Skull Basher, they saw he held something in one hand.

Onua's Golden Mask.

Onua groaned. Ekimu turned to face the

other heroes and said, "Have you learnt nothing?! Skull Basher will defeat you one by one!"

Still at the top of the staircase, Skull Basher placed Onua's Golden Mask over his own face. Onua immediately felt his own energy begin to drain.

Glaring at Skull Basher, Kopaka said, "Let's give him a taste of unity." Kopaka, Gali, Tahu, Lewa, and Pohatu stood close together and drew their weapons. Although Onua remained temporarily immobilized, they felt their elemental energy growing stronger within each one of them. Leaving Ekimu standing beside Onua, they charged up the stairway.

Skull Basher never knew who or what hit him. Knocked off his feet, his body flew back through the tower's entrance, and he dropped Onua's mask as he fell lifeless against the floor.

The heroes recovered Onua's helmet and placed it back on his face. "Thank you, friends," he said as he felt his elemental energy return. Rising from the ground, he lifted his earthquake hammer and said, "Now, let us stop Skull Grinder!"

Ekimu led the heroes into the ancient forge. They moved past Skull Basher's body and proceeded into the main chamber that contained the furnace. The chamber was littered with dusty boxes and shelves stacked with scraps of precious metals as well as ancient tools used for the construction of masks and armor. Ancient masks and weapons hung on the walls. At the far end of the chamber, Skull Grinder stood with his back to the group, facing the immense furnace that was blazing away, kicking off so much heat that it made Tahu feel almost comfortable while making Kopaka feel the opposite.

Skull Grinder turned to face Ekimu and the heroes. In one hand, he clutched a long Mask Stealer Staff with three axe blades, the most feared weapon on the entire island. His other hand held the Golden Mask of Creation, and he appeared to be preparing to toss it into the furnace.

"Too late," said Ekimu. "We will defeat you and get the mask long before it melts."

Skull Grinder laughed. "I will have plenty of time, once I have destroyed you." Lifting the Mask of Creation, he put it on. The entire forge grew suddenly brighter, and Skull Grinder looked as if he was drawing energy from the forge itself.

"Not good," said Ekimu.

Lewa said, "What's the plan?"

"Keep him occupied," Ekimu said as he looked around at the cluttered piles of metal and tools.

Baffled, Gali said, "Is that it?"

"Just fight as long as you can," Ekimu said. He ran over to a stack of boxes containing old, discarded masks and began digging through it, apparently searching for something.

The six heroes looked at each other. As Skull Grinder continued glowing with energy from the forge, the heroes powered up with their own elemental energy. And then they charged him, just as they had charged Skull Basher earlier, except Onua was with them this time. They felt invincible.

But they were no match for the evil wearer of the Mask of Creation. With a single solid swing of his long axe, Skull Grinder slammed the masks off all six heroes. Their masks shattered instantly and fell to the floor. All of the heroes' energy drained and vanished, and they collapsed beside the remains of their broken masks.

Ekimu ignored the brief battle. He was thoroughly preoccupied by some bits and pieces of old tools that he'd found. Hearing Ekimu's aged hands fumbling around in a box of metal parts, Skull Grinder turned, looked at Ekimu, and laughed. The elderly Mask Maker was busily trying to screw a metal handle into another piece that he'd found when Skull Grinder started walking toward him.

Lying on the floor, Kopaka saw Skull Grinder moving straight for Ekimu and muttered, "Must . . . stop him."

"How?" said Gali, who had fallen near Kopaka. "We lost our masks."

The six heroes thought of the Protectors, who had fought so bravely, without any thought of their own safety, and who also had placed so much faith in the Toa. Seeing Skull Grinder step closer to Ekimu, Onua reached out and grabbed Skull Grinder's leg.

"We keep on fighting," Onua said, "as long as we can."

Skull Grinder looked down at Onua with surprise and a mildly annoyed expression. He kicked hard, launching Onua from the floor and sending him slamming against a wall.

Pohatu managed to push himself up from the floor and he grabbed Skull Grinder's arm. Skull Grinder swatted him aside like an insignificant insect. Gali reached for Skull Grinder's other arm and she was also knocked away. Lewa and Kopaka also grabbed for the villain in a desperate effort to slow his progress but he sent them sailing across the chamber, too.

Tahu was the last Toa standing when Ekimu finally found all the pieces that he'd been searching for. Skull Grinder brought his staff down on Tahu, driving the Toa to his knees, and was about to finish him off when he glanced at Ekimu and saw that the Mask Maker had assembled a large hammer.

Ekimu had re-created the Hammer of Power, the same hammer that he had used to defeat Makuta.

He held the hammer high over his old masked head. The hammer glowed and Skull Grinder felt a powerful force rumble through the air. The light from the glowing hammer expanded over Ekimu and his armor, and he was transformed from a frail figure into a powerful warrior.

Ekimu darted toward the startled Skull Grinder. Tahu was still on his knees, and Ekimu jumped up onto his back to gain elevation before he swung his hammer at Skull Grinder's head, knocking the Mask of Creation off Skull Grinder's face.

Skull Grinder collapsed onto the floor. Ekimu caught the Mask of Creation in midair, transferred it to his own face, and the entire chamber exploded with blinding light.

Tahu remained conscious just long enough to see Ekimu's victory. When Tahu passed out, he was still smiling.

## TAHUTA

Tahu didn't know how long he'd been unconscious. Lying on the floor within Ekimu's forge, he was vaguely aware of feeling the heat from the nearby furnace, and believed he had also heard noises that sounded like metal hammering against metal. He wondered if Ekimu was building or fixing something. When he finally opened his eyes, he saw Ekimu holding a Golden Mask for him.

"Wake up, Toa," Ekimu said. "Never have I seen such bravery. You are worthy. Rise!"

Tahu got up and Ekimu placed the mask over his face. As Tahu felt mystical energy rush through his body, he turned to see the other heroes standing before him. Pohatu, Gali, Onua, Kopaka, and Lewa wore Golden Masks, too.

Tahu said, "We are all restored!"

"I still sense evil," Pohatu said. "Makuta is out there somewhere, and his dark powers continue to grow. We must find him and stop him."

Lewa said, "I'm getting the impression that this adventure is far from over."

Gali faced Ekimu and said, "Trust us to save the island. It is our duty. And it is our destiny!"